First published in Great Britain by
HarperCollins *Children's Books* in 2020
HarperCollins *Children's Books* is a division of HarperCollins*Publishers* Ltd,
HarperCollins Publishers
1 London Bridge Street
London SE1 9GF

The HarperCollins website address is
www.harpercollins.co.uk
1

ISBN 978–0–00–830645–8

Ben Fogle and Nikolas Ilic assert the moral right to be identified
as the author and illustrator of the work respectively.

A CIP catalogue record for this title is available from the British Library.

Printed and bound in England by CPI Group (UK) Ltd, Croydon, CR0 4YY

MIX
Paper from
responsible sources
FSC™ C007454

This book is produced from independently certified FSC™ paper
to ensure responsible forest management.

For more information visit: www.harpercollins.co.uk/green

MR DOG

AND THE FARAWAY FOX

BEN FOGLE

with Steve Cole

Illustrated by Nikolas Ilic

HarperCollins *Children's Books*

ankbrook Street

Park

Ryan's house

About the Author

BEN FOGLE is a broadcaster and seasoned adventurer. A modern-day nomad and journeyman, he has travelled to more than a hundred countries and accomplished amazing feats; from swimming with crocodiles to rowing three thousand miles across the Atlantic Ocean; from crossing Antarctica on foot to surviving a year as a castaway on a remote Hebridean island. Most recently, Ben climbed Mount Everest. Oh, and he LOVES dogs.

Books by Ben Fogle

MR DOG AND THE RABBIT HABIT

MR DOG AND THE SEAL DEAL

MR DOG AND A HEDGE CALLED HOG

MR DOG AND THE FARAWAY FOX

To Jack, Josh and Taran

Chapter One

A CRY IN THE NIGHT

It was late in the city. The roads were quiet and the house windows were dark. But not all animals went to bed just because humans did! Nocturnal creatures still roamed the streets and gardens . . .

An eerie sound, like a howling scream, rose up

into the starry springtime blackness of the sky.

Mr Dog jumped awake, his dark eyes wide under their bushy brows. He was a raggedy mutt, with dark scruffy fur, a big black nose and front paws as white as his muzzle. 'What a curious noise,' he said to himself, stretching with a yawn. 'I wonder what it was?'

The short, sad, yowling cry came again. Mr Dog pit-patted across the kitchen to the back

door, stuck his head out through the catflap and raised an ear. He tried to trace the lonely sound.

But the night was quiet again, just the grumble of a car passing in a nearby road, so he went back inside.

Mr Dog didn't often stay in cities. A travelling dog by nature, he preferred fresh air, fields and forests. If he chose to stay with a pet owner, it was usually in a sleepy town or a small-time village. But a little while ago he'd stepped on a thorn and his paw had grown sore. He'd limped into town in search of help.

Luckily, a kind, animal-loving lady called Minnah had found him and taken him home. She'd pulled out the thorn with tweezers, given him a good bath and even washed the red-and-white spotted hanky that he used as a collar! Her

 3

friend, who was a vet, had checked his paw, and luckily the only treatment needed was to soak it in a special bath for ten minutes, twice a day.

'It's feeling much better already,' murmured Mr Dog, waggling his paw. 'And how sweet and clean I smell! I may have to change my name to Lord Dog . . .' He stood on his back paws and tried to look as posh as possible. 'Hmm, perhaps even *Sir* Dog?'

'Sir Silly Dog!' someone giggled from a pet-carrier on the kitchen floor.

'Silly? I'm being serious.' Mr Dog beamed at the tortoise inside the carrier. 'Or *sir*-ious, at least. How are you feeling, Shelly?'

Shelly pushed out her little scaly head. 'I'm feeling glad to have such a noble neighbour!' she said. Shelly was a fifteen-year-old tortoise with a richly patterned shell and a sense of fun that was missing in many tortoises. She was staying with Minnah for a few days while her owners were away. 'I just really hope that someone finds poor old Crawly soon.'

'So do I,' Mr Dog agreed sadly. Crawly was another tortoise who had lived with Shelly for years. Then, two days ago, Crawly had gone missing from their garden. There had been no sign of a forced entry.

'One minute Crawly was there beneath a hedge,' Shelly said, not for the first time, 'and the next minute . . . he was gone.' Shelly's head slowly shrank back inside her shell. 'It all happened so fast.'

'Don't lose hope.' Mr Dog put his nose to the side of the pet-carrier and snuffled Shelly's shell. 'Crawly might still show up, you know . . .'

Suddenly, he heard the creak of a floorboard.

The kitchen light flicked on and Minnah came into the room.

'Hello, boy.' She yawned, patting his head. Mr Dog woofed softly in greeting and wagged his brushy tail.

'That screaming fox woke you up too, did it?' said Minnah, filling the kettle. 'What a racket, calling out like that . . .'

'A fox!' Shelly shivered in her shell – though, of course, Minnah couldn't hear a word she said. 'I never knew that a fox could make a sound like that.'

'Nor me,' Mr Dog agreed. 'Minnah certainly taught us something tonight.'

Shelly's dark eyes twinkled. 'You mean . . . she "*tortoise*" something!'

Mr Dog rolled on to his back and wriggled in amusement. Shelly beamed.

Minnah made herself a cup of tea, and fed Mr Dog a biscuit. Then she switched off the light and went back up to bed.

Mr Dog had just settled himself in his basket when the eerie fox cry sounded again.

'I don't like the thought of a fox being so close by,' Shelly confessed. 'My owner said it could've been a fox who took Crawly from the garden.'

'I hope not,' said Mr Dog, who was a friend to all animals and never one to judge. 'Dogs and foxes tend to avoid each other, so I haven't really met one before . . .'

After a while, Shelly fell asleep, but Mr Dog's ears jumped as the strange howl sounded once more from outside.

I wonder why that fox is calling? thought Mr Dog. *Perhaps it's in trouble. Maybe I can help.* Limping just a little, Mr Dog padded over to the catflap and squeezed through it. *At the very least, I can ask him to keep the noise down so he doesn't disturb the neighbours . . .*

The catflap opened on to a side alley: one way led to the main street, the other to a quiet lane that backed on to a row of garages. The night

was cool and Mr Dog's nose twitched with the

city's scents. The houses were dark, but the

streetlamps cast bright orange patches over the

pavements. Somewhere distant, gulls gave their

rowdy cries and a clock struck three. Mr Dog felt

happy. How nice it was to be outside again!

His nose twitched with a strong, musky smell

from the fir trees that lined someone's garden.

That fox has marked this territory, thought Mr

Dog. *A boy fox, unless I'm very much mistaken. He*

must be close by . . .

Then Mr Dog caught another smell.

The smell of a tortoise!

Quickly he pushed his head through the fir

trees – and couldn't believe his eyes.

A small and scrappy red fox was sitting happily

in the garden – holding a tortoise in its jaws!

Chapter Two

THE FOX FROM FAR AWAY

At the sight of the tortoise in trouble, Mr Dog ran forward, raised his hackles and bared his teeth, a low warning growl building in his throat.

The fox jumped, startled by his arrival, the tortoise still clamped between his teeth.

'Put the tortoise down,' said Mr Dog.

'Oh! Sorry. Do you want to play with it too?'
The fox tossed the tortoise through the air and
it landed on its back beside Mr Dog. 'There you
are! Now you pass it back to me. Go on! Go on!'

Mr Dog ignored the fox, studying the poor
tortoise for injuries. It was still alive, though its
shell was badly scratched. Its back legs looked to
be injured, pulled back in the shell as far as they
would go. An address – *12 Bankbrook Street* – was
written in paint on the underside of the shell.

That's not far from Minnah's house, thought Mr
Dog. Gently, he turned the tortoise the right way
round with his nose.

'Go on, pass it to me!' The fox was almost
bouncing with excitement. 'My name's Ferdy.
What's yours? Come on! I'll give it back, I
promise.'

'This isn't a toy, Ferdy. It's a pet tortoise!'
Mr Dog stood in front of it protectively. 'You've
hurt it.'

'Me?' Ferdy shook his head. 'No! It was like that when I found it!'

'Oh, yes? And where *did* you find it?'

'Round the corner. It was lying in someone's garden,' said Ferdy.

'Well, my name's Mr Dog, and the D-O-G *might* stand for Defender Of Gardens!' He gave Ferdy his sternest look. 'This isn't the wild, you know. You can't go around helping yourself to people's pets.'

'Sorry, Mr Dog. I should've realised it was a pet.' Ferdy looked sad, his moth-eaten tail slunk between his legs. 'I'm an urban fox. I used to live around here, but lately I've been far away.' He

brightened. 'Still, now I'm back in town! Oooh.
Wait. Ooooooh. What do I hear?' He put his ear
to the ground. 'Earthworms! Yum.' Straight away,
Ferdy started digging at the grass, clawing worms
from the muddy hole and guzzling them down.
'Mmm, delicious.'

Mr Dog frowned. 'Ferdy, stop. You're ruining
this lawn!'

Ferdy took no notice, lost in the delight of earthworms. Then Mr Dog's attention was taken as the tortoise started to rock beside him. 'Shelly?' came its croak of a voice. 'Shelly, are you there . . . ?'

'Crawly!' Mr Dog put his nose to the shell. 'Is that you, Crawly?'

'Yes!' Crawly pushed out his frightened head and nodded. 'Oh, what a terrible time I've had! Please, help me!'

Mr Dog carefully picked up the tortoise in his jaws. With a last glare at Ferdy, he carried Crawly through the hedge and then ran back to Minnah's house. His poorly paw throbbed a little, but Mr

Dog didn't slow down. He knew Crawly needed help as soon as possible.

'WUFF! WUFF! WUFF!' Mr Dog barked at the back door and scratched at it with his good front paw until Minnah came down in her dressing gown.

'Oh, boy, however did you get out through that catflap?' she began. Then she saw what Mr Dog was holding. 'Oh, no!'

'It wasn't me!' Mr Dog whined, and put Crawly down at Minnah's feet, then pressed himself against her legs. Minnah quickly scooped up the tortoise and turned on the light. 'Twelve Bankbrook Street,' she read aloud. 'Same address as on Shelly here.' She then looked back down at Mr Dog. 'I don't know what happened out there, boy, but you found Crawly!'

'Mr Dog!' Shelly was up and bright-eyed at the bars of the carry-case. 'You're a genius! You found the old stinker.'

'Cheeky!' Crawly called.

Mr Dog wagged his tail proudly as Minnah fed him a dog treat. Then he curled up in his basket and licked at his paw while his pet owner used her phone to call her vet friend.

'I'm sorry to wake you,' she said. 'I've found that missing tortoise and he's been in the wars. There are some nasty scratches on his shell, but I don't know what made them. There are no teeth marks, but his back legs are hurt. Please, can you come over?'

'Poor Crawly,' said Shelly softly. 'I hope he'll be all right.'

'So do I,' said Mr Dog.

*

Minnah's friend the vet soon arrived. She examined Crawly on Minnah's dining table and confirmed that the tortoise had had a lucky escape. One of his back legs was swollen, and the other looked to be broken.

'I'm sure Crawly will make a full recovery,' the vet said, 'but I'll need to get X-rays before I set

his leg. I'll take him in now.'

'Nice early start for you,' Minnah joked.

'Sorry! What do you think took Crawly?'

'A fox is the most likely suspect.' The vet
smiled down at Mr Dog. 'At least we know who
brought him back! Though how he found him
out there will always be a mystery.'

'I should change my name to *Mystery* Dog,' said Mr Dog with a sleepy smile. But there was one mystery that was keeping him awake: Ferdy the fox. Where had the fox been, so far away? Had he been telling the truth about Crawly being hurt before he'd found him?

If so . . . who had really taken the timid tortoise?

Mr Dog didn't know. But he was determined to find out!

Chapter Three

NEIGHBOURHOOD NUISANCE!

Mr Dog hadn't been asleep for long before a loud and heavy clattering from outside disturbed him. Too tired to investigate this time, he curled up tighter in his basket and went on huffling and puffling.

Later, but still quite early in the morning,

Mr Dog was woken again by angry voices outside.

Minnah had heard them too, and now went out in

her dressing gown to investigate. She left the door

ajar, so an inquisitive Mr Dog slipped out after her.

A small crowd of neighbours had gathered on

the pavement outside the house next door, and

none of them looked happy. Mr Dog realised

what must have caused the clatter. A food-waste

bin, left out for collection on the driveway, had

been thrown on its side and dragged all about, its

lid forced open and the messy contents scattered

over the front garden, the pavement and the road.

'Fox!' said a bald man with a red face. 'It has to

be a fox that did this to my bin.'

An old lady nodded. 'I've seen one about. The filthy thing's dug holes in my garden.'

'And I heard a tortoise went missing just round the corner,' said a younger woman. 'That's got to be a fox.'

'They're known for it,' Minnah agreed. 'We found the poor thing, but it's been hurt, and had to go to the vet . . .'

Mr Dog sniffed the air for traces of Ferdy's scent. He knew foxes were frequent scent-markers, and sure enough he caught a faint whiff. There was a much stronger smell of leftover lasagne on the pavement, but he supposed that now was not the time to start cleaning up the mess in his own special way.

'I've got rabbits in my back garden,' the bald man said. 'If I catch a fox bothering them, the law says I'm allowed to shoot it!'

Minnah looked shocked. 'You can't! It's only obeying its nature. Wherever there are people, there will be foxes. Just like there will always be rats and gulls and pigeons.'

'But foxes are bigger,' the old lady said. 'They can bite. They're dangerous!'

The other neighbours nodded and muttered.

'If you see it again, call me,' said the bald man. 'I'll come right round to deal with it!'

Minnah shook her head sadly. She started to pick up the rubbish and put it back in the bin.

The younger woman gave her a hand. Mr Dog picked up some lasagne – just to help out.

I hope that Ferdy stops causing trouble around here, thought Mr Dog. *If he doesn't, I don't like to think what might happen!*

*

Later that day, Mr Dog was delighted when Crawly was brought back to Minnah's house. The vet had set the tortoise's little leg in a splint and an impressive white bandage was wrapped round his shell to help hold the splint in place. The other leg had been patched up, and Crawly was able to hobble across the kitchen floor at quite a speed.

'Crawly!' said Shelly. 'You're back.'

'What about my back?' joked Crawly. 'It's my

leg you should be asking after!'

The two tortoises spent a full minute in silent

laughter.

'You're a very brave tortoise, Crawly,' said Mr Dog. 'Do you remember what happened to you?'

Crawly shifted uncomfortably. 'Something grabbed me, and lifted me into the air. It was moving so fast! The next thing I remember, it was dark and I was looking up at a fox. It picked me up and threw me!'

'A fox!' Shelly nodded her scaly head. 'I knew it.'

'That fox said that he *didn't* steal you,' said Mr Dog thoughtfully. 'He only found you in a garden.'

'He must be a fibbing fox!' said Crawly.

'Perhaps,' said Mr Dog, 'but you were gone for a long time, Crawly. Why didn't the fox get bored and eat you up?'

'Eeek!' Crawly pulled his head back into his shell and stayed there.

Shelly thought hard. 'If the fox didn't take Crawly, then who did?'

'I haven't the Mr Foggiest!' said Mr Dog. 'Ferdy didn't strike me as an aggressive fox. He seemed very friendly indeed. And if there *is* a mean animal doing things round here, I don't want the neighbours blaming an innocent fox and hurting him.'

'So what will you do?' asked Shelly.

'Find him and tell him to stay far away,' Mr Dog decided. 'That way he can be safe.'

'But what about you?' said Shelly. 'If you're out at night alone with a mean animal on the loose . . . you won't be safe at all!'

*

Mr Dog rested his paw all day. He ate a hearty meal of kibble that evening, and scraps from Minnah's plate too. He knew he would need all his energy for a night on the trail of Ferdy the fox!

Once Minnah had gone to bed, Mr Dog squeezed out through the catflap again and into the night. His nose twitched. He couldn't smell Ferdy nearby. He couldn't smell any other foxes either.

I'll go back to the place where I met him last night and try to pick up the trail from there, thought Mr Dog.

The garden was still covered in holes. Mr Dog sniffed again: Ferdy's scent was getting stronger. 'The nose knows!' he chuckled, and carried along the street, turning his head this way and that. Yes, he had the scent now for sure! He quickened his step and turned into a driveway that ran down the side of a house. He followed it through a gate that stood ajar and into an overgrown back garden.

And then he stopped.

The back door to the house stood open.

There were lights on inside. Through the lounge window, he saw a man sitting on the sofa watching television.

Mr Dog looked around the garden and sniffed again. Where had Ferdy gone?

Suddenly, he heard an almighty shriek from upstairs. 'Oh, NO!' a young boy yelled. 'There's a fox up here!'

Mr Dog's ears flew up. 'So *that's* where Ferdy is,' he breathed. 'That crazy fox has gone inside the house!'

Chapter Four

A FRIGHT IN THE GARDEN

Mr Dog watched from the garden as the man in the lounge jumped up, grabbed a broom from the kitchen and ran upstairs. 'Where is that fox?'

A door slammed, and the boy's frightened voice could be heard: 'I've shut it in the bedroom, Dad.'

'I'll get it out!' said the man.

Oh, dear, thought Mr Dog. *I don't know why Ferdy went into someone's house, but he could get badly hurt!* With a few woofs to the patron saint of scruffy but well-meaning dogs, Mr Dog bounded into the house and raced up the stairs.

The dad had thrown open the door, holding the broom like a club. Ferdy was cowering in a corner of the room, wide-eyed and terrified.

'WOOF!' Mr Dog jumped up at the dad and his paws pushed him into the bedroom. The dad went staggering forward. As he did so, Ferdy ducked through his legs and bolted past Mr Dog,

back out on to the landing. The boy screamed

again. Mr Dog herded Ferdy back down the

stairs.

'Wait a minute,' said Ferdy, going into the

kitchen. 'I smell something nice.'

'What?' Mr Dog stared in amazement as Ferdy

stopped to grab the remains of a roast chicken

from the kitchen table. Already the man with the

broom was running back downstairs. 'Come on,

Ferdy, we have to go!'

Mr Dog ran into the garden and Ferdy raced

after him with the carcass in his jaws.

'This way!' hissed the fox, heading for the fence at the back of the garden. Mr Dog saw a hole had been dug there.

'I'll get you, you vermin!' the dad bellowed, waving his broom.

Ferdy slipped through the hole with ease, his scruffy tail disappearing with a flourish. Mr Dog tried to squeeze after him, but the hole was too small! The dad was getting closer. Mr Dog dug deeper and finally managed to drag himself through into the next garden. He lay on the dark lawn, panting for breath.

'First thing in the morning, I'm blocking this hole!' the dad said from the other side of the fence. 'And I'll fix the catch on that back door right now . . .' He turned and stomped away.

'Ferdy?' Mr Dog whispered. 'Where are you?'

'Here!' Ferdy's head popped up happily from a flowerbed and he dropped the chicken carcass. 'Thanks for your help back there, dog. Weird, huh? Why were those two humans so shouty?'

'I'll tell you why.' Mr Dog padded over to join him. 'They were shouty because a wild animal just walked into their private property uninvited! They were scared of you.'

'But why? I was only seeing if they had any food.' Ferdy frowned. 'Ryan used to feed me all the time.'

41

'Who's Ryan?' said Mr Dog.

'A man. He was my friend,' said Ferdy. 'He was cool.'

Mr Dog raised his bushy brows. 'He fed you?'

'Yes! I used to visit Ryan every night. Sometimes he would feed me right from his hand!' Ferdy grinned at the memory. 'After a while, Ryan just left his front door open so I could wander in and say hello . . .'

'I see.' Mr Dog felt suddenly sad. He understood now why Ferdy would wander into a stranger's house without fear. Ryan had started to tame this urban fox. He had given food freely and encouraged Ferdy to enter his home. Now Ferdy thought that all humans were friendly and that it was safe to approach them for food or shelter. He was wrong.

'Ferdy, you must listen to me. Not everyone in town likes foxes as much as Ryan. You can't just . . .' Mr Dog stopped talking, puzzled. Ferdy had started digging up the flowerbed, scattering soil and blooms all over the place. 'Whatever are you doing now?'

'Don't mind me.' Ferdy picked up the chicken carcass again and dropped it into the hole. 'I'm just burying this roast chicken.'

'What?' Mr Dog shook his head. 'Why would you do that?'

'We foxes like to know we have a spare meal in reserve,' Ferdy explained, filling the hole with mud. 'I have secret dinners buried all over this neighbourhood.'

Mr Dog held up a paw to stop him. 'If you have more food than you need, then why did you knock over a food bin last night?'

Ferdy blinked. 'I didn't, Mr Dog.'

'Are you sure?' said Mr Dog. 'You dig holes in people's gardens, you take from their houses, you steal tortoises . . .'

'I told you I *found* that

tortoise!' Ferdy insisted. 'I only wanted to play with it.'

'That tortoise was badly hurt!' Mr Dog said sternly. 'Your behaviour is upsetting a lot of people, Ferdy.'

'But I'm a fox!' Ferdy protested. 'How do people expect me to behave?'

'They're not really sure.' Mr Dog tried to explain. 'Humans often forget that the world around them is wild. They build towns and cities and don't think of the animals

 45

there. And if those animals cause problems, they try to get rid of them.' He gave Ferdy a smile. 'You said you'd been far away. Perhaps you should go back there for a while till things calm down?'

'No! Don't say that!' Ferdy looked upset. 'I'm never going far away again. You're a nasty dog to say that I should.' He turned his back on Mr Dog and ran away into the night.

'Ferdy, wait!' Mr Dog tried to chase after the fox, but his paw was stinging from his desperate digging.

Ferdy had gone.

With a sigh, Mr Dog went back to the hole in

the fence and carefully wriggled under and into

the dark garden. Then he squeezed through the

gate and sadly headed home.

Chapter Five

ATTACK IN THE ALLEYWAY

Mr Dog walked back slowly. It was nearly midnight, and the streets of the city were quiet. Mr Dog retreated into shadowy alleyways whenever he spotted people – he didn't want anyone reporting a stray dog on the loose!

He'd just reached the street where Minnah

lived when he heard a group of people walking his way. Mr Dog ducked down a dark alley between two houses and waited for them to pass.

Then he heard a kerfuffle behind him. He couldn't see through the darkness but he heard a clatter of claws, and a loud bang as something fell over. The smell of soggy leftovers covered the scent of the culprit.

It's another food-bin attack! Mr Dog realised. His hackles rose and he took a step further into the shadows. 'Who's there?' he growled.

Suddenly, he caught a whiff of fox . . .

The next thing Mr Dog knew, something was rushing towards him out of the darkness.

It charged him
aside, and he found
himself thrown
against the wall.
Shocked and
shaken, Mr Dog
rolled over and
jumped up with a
bark. *What hit me?*
he thought. Then
he caught a glimpse
of something small
and furry trotting
down the alley

towards him from the direction of the street.

Mr Dog woofed in surprise. 'Ferdy?'

'Hello!' said Ferdy brightly, coming closer.

Just then a door handle turned and a light flicked on. A side door to the house swung open to reveal a frowning woman. She stared at the food all over the ground . . . at Mr Dog, looking up at her and wagging his tail as fast as it would go . . . and then she saw Ferdy.

'AAAAGH! A fox!' The woman took a step back inside her house.

'Hello!' Ferdy said brightly, trotting up to her without fear. 'Do you have any food for a friendly fox?'

The woman couldn't understand him, of course. All she saw was a fox prancing straight towards her – and she screamed as loudly as she could!

Mr Dog jumped in front of the fox, blocking his path. 'Come on, Ferdy, we'd better go. The D-O-G part of my name is short for "DO Get a shift on!"'

The dog and the fox ran from the alleyway, back into the street. The woman screamed again. Lights were coming on at the windows of the houses close by. Mr Dog and Ferdy hid inside some bushes, panting for breath.

'I must admit, I didn't expect to see you again tonight,' said Mr Dog.

'I came after you to apologise,' said Ferdy.
'I know you were only trying to help me. I
shouldn't have gone off in a huff like that.'

'You shouldn't have gone up to that lady,
either,' Mr Dog told him. 'The neighbours will
not be pleased.'

'The lady might have been friendly,' Ferdy
argued. 'Like Ryan was.'

'But she wasn't. I tried to tell you – a lot of
people are scared of foxes.' Mr Dog put a paw on
his. 'However, I am very pleased that you came
along. I think you scared off whatever attacked
me down that alley. Did you see what it was?'

'No,' said Ferdy. 'I think it was grey . . . or

maybe white . . . the size of a cat . . . or an

oversized rat . . .'

'And it vanished into thin air,' said Mr Dog

thoughtfully. 'Well, whatever it is, I suspect that

you will be taking the blame for its latest actions.'

He frowned, and his ears drooped. 'Come to

think of it, so will I!'

'You should come with me

to find Ryan,' said Ferdy.

'He looked after me

before. He will look after

me again, I just know it.'

He threw back his head

and screamed his eerie cry.

'I'm just asking any other foxes who might know where he is.'

'It's hard to find just one person in a city,' said Mr Dog. 'He might have moved far away.'

'Don't say "far away",' said Ferdy. He snorted sadly. 'I *hate* far away.'

'But why?' asked Mr Dog.

'I told you. I've been far away and I didn't like it.' Ferdy sighed. 'On the journey there, I thought it would be fun. But it wasn't.'

The two animals lay down in silence for a while, until the lights in the houses went dark again, and the woman had cleaned up the food that had spilled from her bin. They made a funny pair, the dark dog and the ginger fox, huddled together in the undergrowth with four white paws between them.

Finally, the street was silent again. Mr Dog stuck out his sizable nose from the bushes, checking the way was clear.

His nostrils caught the scent of *another* fox. A fox who was very close by . . .

'Hey.' An old foxy face pushed through the bushes. His ginger fur was flecked with silver, and a scar ran down from his right eye. 'I heard screaming.' He looked at Ferdy. 'Was that you, boy? You want information, is that right?'

'Yes, sir,' said Ferdy.

'Well, Old Foxy Loxie knows a lot of things.
And what he doesn't know, he can find out . . .'
The sly old face smiled a yellow-toothed smile.
'For a price.'

Mr Dog was wary. 'What sort of a price?'

'Food. Scraps. Chickens.' Old Foxy Loxie
dribbled with delight. 'Mmm, I love me some
chickens.'

'I just buried some roast chicken scraps,' said Ferdy. 'If you can find my human friend Ryan for me, they're yours.'

'I'd do ANYTHING for chicken,' said Old Foxy Loxie. 'You got yourself a deal, kid.' He threw back his head and gave the same sort of eerie scream that Mr Dog had heard a lot of lately. 'I'll get back to you.'

With that, the old fox pulled his face out of the bushes and slunk away.

'Well, that's a promising lead,' said Mr Dog.

Ferdy grinned. 'I knew stealing the roast chicken from that house was a good idea!'

'It was a terrible idea!' Mr Dog told him. Then

he sighed. Ferdy just didn't have a clue about how to stay safe around humans. 'Anyway, I'd better start heading back home. I hope Old Foxy Loxie can help you. In the meantime, do you think you can stay out of trouble?'

'I'll try.' Ferdy grinned and sniffed the air. 'OOOH! I can smell earthworms again.' Straight away, he started digging up the lawn beside the bushes.

'Not now! It's someone's garden!' Mr Dog shook his head. 'Go on, get away from here . . . and good luck!'

Chapter Six

ACROSS THE ROAD OF DOOM

Mr Dog made it home and sneaked back inside the catflap without waking anyone, even the tortoises.

Shelly and Crawly's owner, Dan, came to collect them the next morning. He had already heard talk of last night's fox sighting.

'Yasmin at number twenty-two told me the animal came right up to her door, bold as brass!' Dan said. 'She says it was ready to attack her. But she screamed and scared it off.'

What rot! thought Mr Dog, growling quietly.

Dan looked down at him. 'She said that she also saw a dog that looked like you last night . . .'

Mr Dog looked up at him with his widest eyes as if to say, *Who, me?*

'I'm sure it wasn't my poorly boy here,' said Minnah firmly. 'He's a hero. We'd never have found Crawly without him!'

'That's true.' Dan gave Mr Dog a stroke on the head. 'Well, Minnah, I'm going to add extra fencing round my garden and put chicken wire into the soil around it so nothing else can burrow through. My tortoises will be safe and secure from now on.'

'A tortoise loves *shell*-ter,' joked Shelly, and Crawly chortled happily.

Mr Dog gave a yap of farewell as the tortoises were taken away in their carry-cases.

Minnah saw Dan to the door, said goodbye to Shelly and Crawly, then came back to Mr Dog in the kitchen. 'I hope it *wasn't* you outside last night,' Minnah said. 'Still, your paw does look a little bit sore again. I think I'm going to board up the catflap, just in case.'

Mr Dog sighed. *I'm a prisoner!*

While he was grateful to Minnah for all she'd done, he couldn't help but envy Ferdy roaming free in the city. He hoped the fox would stay out of trouble.

That night, he was just drifting off into dreams of chasing invisible animals down alleyways when he heard a scuffling at the catflap. His ears twitched, and a growl started to build in his furry throat.

Then he heard a quiet voice call from outside: 'Mr Dog? It's me, Ferdy.'

'Ferdy!' Mr Dog frowned and crossed quickly to the catflap. 'My dear old chap, what are you doing?'

'I'm pulling off the wood that's blocking this flap in the door so you can come out.' Ferdy was panting with excitement. 'Old Foxy Loxie has found Ryan's new home, here in the city. He gave me directions, and I gave him the roast chicken I buried. But I'm scared I'll get into trouble again by myself.' Ferdy whined softly. 'Will you come with me?'

Mr Dog hesitated. He knew that Minnah didn't want him to go outside. But then it wasn't his fault if the catflap covering had been pulled down, was it?

'Of course I'll come with you.' Mr Dog smiled. 'Let's go!'

*

Ferdy led Mr Dog through the streets into an unfamiliar part of the city. 'Old Foxy Loxie was pretty sure that Ryan lives on the other side of the Road of Doom,' he said brightly.

'The Road of Doom?' Mr Dog bunched his bushy eyebrows. 'I don't like the sound of that!'

Ferdy moved on through the city with a fox's speed and stealth, flitting along the streets like a small red shadow. When someone came in sight, he would pause behind a parked car or a tree, then dart across to the next piece of cover he spied. Mr Dog did his best to keep up. His paw was feeling better for the extra soak he'd been given, but, all the same, he tried to step on it as lightly as he could.

As houses gave way to office buildings, Mr Dog became aware of a roaring, whooshing noise getting louder in his floppy ears. 'Cars,' he muttered. 'Lots and lots of cars.'

Ferdy squeezed under some railings. There

was a very wide road on the other side with another line of railings running down the middle. Mr Dog counted three lanes on one side and three more on the other. Cars were whizzing past in both directions. Their headlights dazzled his eyes.

'This must be your Road of Doom,' said Mr Dog. 'A big main road! It's not safe to cross here. The humans will have a footbridge, or some funny black-and-white stripes to walk on somewhere ...'

'You're such a pet!' said Ferdy. 'I'm sure it'll be fine.'

With that, he dashed straight out into the road!

'Ferdy!' Mr Dog howled. He was about to rush after the fox when a truck came zooming past in front of him! Dust blew in his face. Another car quickly followed, blocking Mr Dog's view. He heard a squeal of brakes and the angry *beep-beep* of a horn as a motorbike swerved sharply and the driver almost lost control. Horrified, Mr Dog saw that Ferdy was about to cross the third and final lane. The little fox hadn't noticed a coach hurtling towards him . . .

Woofing a warning, Mr Dog timed his dash with split-second skill. He dashed straight across the road and nipped Ferdy on the bottom! With a yelp, the fox flew forward with Mr Dog hot

on his heels. The coach barely missed them! It thundered past with a rush of wind that almost knocked the animals over.

'That was a reckless thing to do, Ferdy!' cried Mr Dog. 'You must ALWAYS take special care around roads.'

Ferdy looked shaken. 'Why didn't anyone stop for us?'

'They weren't expecting you to run out in front of them like that,' Mr Dog explained. 'You could have caused a terrible accident.' He softened his voice. 'Even so. I do hope I didn't hurt your bottom too badly.'

'I'll live,' said Ferdy with a sheepish smile.

'Thanks to you, Mr Dog.'

'*Missed-a-Coach* might be a better name right now,' said Mr Dog with a big doggy grin of relief.

He waited for a safe break in the traffic before leading Ferdy carefully across to the other side of the Road of Doom. Ferdy sneezed and snorted to clear his snout of traffic fumes, then led the way once more through the city's maze of streets.

'I've got Ryan's scent!' Ferdy said, his tail flicking about with excitement. He scampered across a small square park with play equipment, surrounded by houses on all sides. 'He's around here somewhere . . .'

'Not so fast,' came a low growl behind them.

Mr Dog turned to find another fox skulking out from behind a slide. She was bigger than Ferdy, with a grey belly, and had one fang missing. He gulped. This new arrival did *not* look like a fox who enjoyed a pleasant chat.

Menacingly, she stalked towards Ferdy and Mr Dog . . .

Chapter Seven

A LONG WAY TO SAY GOODBYE

'My name's Vix,' the tough fox told Ferdy with a sniff. 'This is my patch. What are you doing out with a soppy pet dog?'

'I'm not a pet!' Mr Dog protested. 'I'm a dog of the road.'

'The Road of Doom,' Ferdy added proudly.

'He helped me to cross it.'

'A dog that helps foxes, eh?' Vix looked Mr Dog up and down. 'You must want something badly if you crossed the Road of Doom for it.'

'We're looking for a human called Ryan,' said Mr Dog. 'A friend to foxes.'

'Aha! The human guy Old Foxy Loxie was asking about?' Vix narrowed her eyes. 'Well, I know this Ryan character. But he's *not* very friendly.'

'He'll be friendly to me,' said Ferdy. 'Can you show us where he lives?'

'Maybe,' said Vix. She walked up to Ferdy. 'Say, "Please, great Vix."'

'Please, Vix grates!' said Mr Dog slyly. 'Er, is that close enough?'

Vix narrowed her eyes.

'If you tell us where Ryan is, I'll think you're *really* great.' Ferdy gave her a playful nip on the muzzle. 'C'mon. Tell Ferdy!'

Vix stared at Ferdy for a few seconds. Mr Dog held his breath.

Finally, she smiled and pointed a paw. 'Ryan lives in that box of bricks over there. Red door.'

'Ooh! Yes! Ooh! I see his van parked outside.' Ferdy gave her an excited lick on the ear. 'Thanks, Vix. Come on, Mr Dog!'

Mr Dog bowed his head politely to Vix, and followed Ferdy. The brash fox had gone bounding up to the red door. He scratched at it, snuffling and yapping. 'Ryan! Ryan, are you there?'

Mr Dog held back by the bushes at the front of the house, watching. A light came on behind the door. Ferdy pranced about impatiently. Then the door opened a little.

'No way! I don't believe it,' came a man's voice from behind the door. 'It's that fox again!'

'Who?' came a woman's voice from inside the house.

'The fox I used to feed,' said Ryan. 'I told you about him, remember? I don't believe it . . . he's come back!'

'That's right, Ryan!' said Ferdy happily. 'I knew you didn't mean to lose me so far away!'

'What?' Mr Dog gasped. 'It was *Ryan* who took you far away?'

'Well, yes. He took me in his van.' Ferdy

looked sad. 'I'm sure it was just a game. He didn't mean to lose me . . . and now I've found my way back.'

The door opened. Ferdy beamed with happiness as a man stepped out on to the doorstep. 'Ryan!'

Of course, Ryan couldn't understand a word that Ferdy was saying – and it seemed he didn't want to. 'Go away!' he hissed, and clapped his hands in the Ferdy's face. 'Scram, fox. Get out of here!'

Ferdy jumped and scurried back a few paces. 'I . . . I don't understand. Ryan . . . ?'

'You've got me into enough trouble,' Ryan said, shooing Ferdy away. 'Leave me alone!'

Mr Dog watched in confusion. The man clearly knew Ferdy, so why was he acting so unkindly?

The woman that Ryan had called came to the door. 'What are you doing? Oh!' She dropped her voice to a whisper as she saw Ferdy. 'Isn't he lovely?'

Ferdy stared back at her, a hopeful look in his eyes.

'You really used to feed this fox by hand?' the woman went on.

'Yes.' Ryan looked unhappy. 'I encouraged him to come to me. Fed him. Even let him sit on my sofa. Problem was, he expected the same treatment from my neighbours. He'd run up to them, leave a mess in their gardens, yowl outside half the night . . .' He sighed. 'The neighbours said they'd get rid of him. For his own sake I had to take him away. So I lured him into the van and drove off with him.'

'Poor Ferdy,' murmured Mr Dog.

'I drove for seventy miles, took him to some woods and set him free,' Ryan went on. 'I know foxes have an amazing sense of direction, but I never expected he'd find his way back here.'

'You were my friend,' Ferdy said softly.

The woman looked at Ryan. 'Is that why you moved away?' she asked. 'In case he came back?'

'No! After I got that fox out of the way, other foxes took over his territory. The neighbours blamed me. They wanted me to pay for garden repairs and stuff . . . so I shifted over here.'

The woman laughed. 'And now he's found you anyway.'

'Well, he can un-find me again,' said Ryan firmly. 'I'm not encouraging foxes any more. Go on, shoo.' He waved his arms again. 'Find someone else to feed you. Go!'

Ferdy turned, lowered his head and stalked away. Mr Dog went after him. Behind them, the red front door quietly closed.

'Ferdy!' Mr Dog called. 'Wait. I'm sorry you came such a long way just to say goodbye.'

'It's not your fault,' said Ferdy. 'I didn't know I was being a pest. Maybe I *should* have stayed far away after all . . .' He sighed. 'Trouble was, I didn't like the woods. Everything was too quiet and wide open.'

'That's because you're a city fox!' Vix emerged from behind a nearby wheelie bin. 'You belong here, little guy.'

'I don't think I belong anywhere,' said Ferdy

sadly. 'Not here *or* far away.' He looked at Mr

Dog. 'Thanks for coming with me. I'm sorry it

was a waste of time. I'll walk back with you and

I'll push the boards back against your flap in the

door, so you don't get into trouble.'

Mr Dog hesitated. He wasn't sure it was wise

for Ferdy to show his foxy face in Minnah's

neighbourhood again. But he didn't want to

say no to the poor fox after what he'd just been

through.

'I would enjoy your company,' Mr Dog said

grandly.

Vix smiled, showing her single fang. 'Enjoy

your road trip, dogs.'

'There'll be no more trips across the Road of Doom,' said Mr Dog firmly. 'This time we will find a footbridge!'

Chapter Eight

THE CULPRIT REVEALED!

Mr Dog and Ferdy found a footbridge for a much safer crossing. They walked in silence across the city, kept company by the rumble of traffic and the cries of gulls overhead.

Finally, Mr Dog reached the quiet dark lane that stretched past the back gardens on Minnah's street. On one side, a row of old garages backed on to the lane. On the other side stood wooden fences guarding the gardens. Narrow alleyways ran between the houses, connecting the lane to the main road.

'Here we are, then,' said Mr Dog. He smiled at Ferdy. 'Thanks for walking me back.'

'I'll leave now.' Ferdy traipsed sadly away along the lane. 'I know you don't want me messing things up for you.'

'It's not that!' said Mr Dog, going after him. 'I'm only worried that you'll be in danger if you stay here.'

'Sure.' Ferdy hung his head. 'Bye.' He turned

into the next alleyway, heading for the main road.

'Wait!' Mr Dog followed him into the alley

and scampered past him, blocking the way.

'Ferdy, I know it's not easy being a fox in the city.

But you can't just give up.'

'What else can I do?' said Ferdy. 'I'm going to

go far, far away. No one will ever see me again—!'

Suddenly, the bloodcurdling hiss of an angry

cat came from the alleyway.

'MIAOWWWWWWWW!'

Mr Dog's hackles rose and he gasped as a large white cat came racing out of the darkness, clearly terrified. It ran past Mr Dog and Ferdy, and turned left down the lane, vanishing into the night.

Ferdy stared, wide-eyed. 'What spooked that cat?'

'I don't know.'

Mr Dog edged deeper

into the alleyway

to investigate . . .

Once again, something fierce and fast-

moving burst out of the darkness and came

clattering towards him!

Mr Dog's jaw dropped in surprise as his

attacker was

revealed in the orange

glow of a streetlamp.

It was a bird! A bird that was almost as big as

he was.

Her head and belly were white while her

wings were grey, and her tail feathers striped

with black. Her beak was like a curved yellow

hook.

'She's a gull!' barked Mr Dog. 'An enormous

herring gull!'

The gull burst into angry flight again. She

brought up her orange claws and thudded into Mr

Dog's side. Poor Mr Dog was bowled over sideways.

The gull shrieked, ready to attack again. But Ferdy darted towards the gull, blocking its way and baring his teeth. The gull squawked and retreated back into the alley shadows, hopping over Mr Dog.

Why doesn't she just fly away? Mr Dog

wondered. Then he saw that one of the gull's wings was sticking out at a strange angle.

'Her wing is broken!' Mr Dog realised. 'That's why she was so low to the ground when she flew at me. She's injured.'

Ferdy frowned. 'If she's broken her wing, why would she risk attacking healthy animals?'

'No idea,' Mr Dog admitted. 'You would think she'd want to stay out of trouble . . .'

The light outside the house went on as its owner came to investigate the noise. In the sharp white light, Mr Dog could see the large gull huddling now against the long line of garages. Tucked into a hole in the brickwork near the top

of the wall was a mess of sticks and straw. Mr
Dog saw a small downy head pop up into sight.

'This gull has a chick in her nest!' Mr
Dog realised. 'So *that's* why she was being so
aggressive. She knocked over bins to get food
because she couldn't catch her own. The poor
thing is only trying to protect her young!'

The alleyway grew brighter still as the back
door swung open. Mr Dog recognised the old
woman who'd been so cross about foxes before.
She looked at Ferdy. 'You! Fox!' she gasped. 'Just
you stay there . . .'

With that, she ran back into the house.

Mr Dog frowned for a moment – and then

gasped as he remembered the gathering of neighbours after the bin had been knocked over the day before. When the old lady had said she didn't like foxes, the bald man had answered: *'If you see it again, call me. I'll be right round to deal with it!'*

'Ferdy,' said Mr Dog urgently. 'You must go, right now.' He tried to nudge Ferdy along the alley, but the fox dodged and scampered past him, getting closer to the gull. She screeched and picked something up from the gutter with her beak. The next moment, she flapped her good wing enough to leave the ground and tossed whatever she was holding at them. Something

bounced off the concrete;

something yellow and black and

shaped like a semicircle.

Mr Dog gasped. It was a tortoise!

'Mr Dog?' A familiar scaly head

peeped out from inside. '*Sir* Dog!

Help me, please!'

'Shelly?' Mr Dog couldn't believe

his eyes. 'First Crawly was taken,

now you?'

'That gull stole me from the garden!' Shelly cried. 'She must be the one who took Crawly too. When she lost him, she came back to the garden looking for him – and took me instead!'

'Well, I'll be . . .' Mr Dog gave Ferdy his biggest, doggiest grin. 'The neighbours have got it all backwards. You really *did* just find Crawly the other night! You took him from that gull and saved him from becoming bird food.'

'I *told* you I found him,' said Ferdy.

'Uh-oh,' said Mr Dog as the bald man suddenly came puffing into sight from a few doors down in his dressing gown. 'Convincing this person might prove more difficult.'

'There you are, you wild menace!' The bald man ran into the alleyway and pulled an air pistol from his dressing-gown pocket. 'Hold still, fox . . .'

He aimed the gun.

Chapter Nine

HAPPY ENDINGS?

'NO!' Mr Dog barked his scariest bark and
hurled himself at the bald man. The man
staggered back, dropped the pistol and fell over
on to his bottom. Mr Dog jumped over Shelly,
picked up the pistol and threw it away with
a flick of his head. The pistol went skittering

towards the gull and gave it a fright. It took off into awkward flight again, screeching.

'That gull's a monster!' cried the bald man.

The old lady had opened the back door again. She saw all the kerfuffle in the alleyway and gasped as the huge gull tried to pick up the tortoise from the ground once more. But Ferdy ran up to her, barking and yowling, doing his best to defend Shelly. The gull screeched and pecked at him, but Ferdy stood his ground, yapping and yipping.

'He's trying to help!' The old lady realised. 'Maybe the fox isn't so bad after all.'

'There's no "maybe" about it,' said Mr Dog

proudly. He jumped up and gave his scariest growl. Between the two of them, the dog and the fox frightened the gull away. She backed off, puffing up her feathers. Finally, with a screech, she turned and hopped nearer to the nest. The chick was still bobbing its fluffy head about.

The mother gull glared at her audience, as if daring them to come any closer to her offspring.

Now Mr Dog turned to the fallen tortoise and nudged him towards the bald man.

The bald man scooped up Shelly from the ground and squinted in the glare from the outside light. 'She looks all right. I don't think she's been hurt.'

'I tucked everything in,' Shelly said proudly.

'Well done, Shelly!' Mr Dog woofed. 'And well done, Ferdy too.'

Ferdy looked nervous. 'Should I run away now? Are the humans going to try to get me again?' The sound of footsteps made him nudge closer to Mr Dog. 'Someone *else* is coming . . .'

'It's all right,' said Mr Dog, wagging his tail. 'She's a friend.'

'What a lot of noise,' cried Minnah. 'It woke me up!' She had arrived in her pyjamas with a coat over the top, and her frown deepened at the sight of Mr Dog. 'I thought I heard your woofing. How on earth did you get out this time . . . ?'

Mr Dog beat his tail even harder and woofed

again, turning in a circle while Minnah took in the astonishing scene.

'A gull with a bad wing!' Minnah exclaimed. 'A very tame fox . . . And is that Shelly the tortoise?'

'What a night!' The old lady smiled from her doorstep. 'I reckon we could all use a cup of tea.'

'You can come to mine.' Minnah took Shelly from the bald man and smiled at Ferdy. 'All of you can.'

*

Soon Minnah's kettle was boiling in the kitchen while she spoke to the vet on the telephone. Shelly was shaken but snug in a carry-case, munching on lettuce.

'Are you sure you're okay?' asked Mr Dog.

'I'm better than okay,' Shelly said. 'Crawly's been going on and on about his adventures . . . and now I can go on about my adventures too!'

'Adventures are quite marvellous things,' Mr Dog agreed. 'Provided they have a happy ending of course.'

He smiled as he padded through to the lounge. Beyond the patio doors he could see Ferdy in the garden, curled up beside a tree. He had dozed off after his busy night.

'Just because this fox didn't knock over those bins doesn't mean another one won't,' the bald man said, 'and foxes do steal tortoises. Same as they kill chickens.'

'They're hunting animals. They don't understand our rules.' Minnah had come in and passed the bald man a mug of tea. 'Foxes get confused by human behaviour. They don't know what's okay and what's not because different people react differently to them. And small wonder, since so many myths have been made up about them.'

'That's a terrible *myth*-take,' joked Mr Dog, and was rewarded with a tortoise giggle from the carry-case.

The bald man said nothing, but the old lady

was nodding her head. 'I suppose it's easy to forget that animals are just like us,' she said. 'Take that gull, for instance. If your child was hungry, wouldn't you do anything you could to feed it? If you were hurt and couldn't get help, wouldn't you be in a bad mood too?'

The bald man shrugged. 'I suppose so.'

Minnah nodded and looked out at Ferdy. 'We all have to share this city. And we should share it kindly with the animals that call it home.'

'Woof!'

Mr Dog agreed.

'Ha! You're funny, boy.' Minnah smiled at him. 'It's almost like you understand us!'

Mr Dog wagged his tail innocently.

'Well, anyway,' said Minnah. 'The vet is on her way over again. I don't think she's delighted with yet another early house call! But she said she would report that poor gull to a wildlife rescue charity. They'll be able to give her and her chick the help they need.'

'I am glad,' said the old lady. 'Do you think we should check on the fox too?'

Minnah nodded and led the way into the garden. Mr Dog scampered out in front of her.

Ferdy yawned and opened his eyes. Finding

himself surrounded by people he jumped, spooked. 'Mr Dog?' he whined. 'Is everything all right?'

'I think it's going to be,' said Mr Dog.

'Sure. For everyone except me,' said Ferdy. 'I can't stay here. Humans are too confusing! It's time I left.'

With that, the fox turned and slunk away into the night.

'Foxes may act tame sometimes,' Minnah mused. 'But they'll always be wild at heart.'

'Yes, they will,' muttered Mr Dog. 'Hmmm. Perhaps, somehow, I need to get Ferdy to remember that!'

Chapter Ten

WILD AT HEART

The sun was rising as the vet finished checking Shelly and gave her a clean bill of health.

'I've heard of gulls stealing tortoises from gardens if they're desperate enough,' she said. 'They drop them from a height to try to break them open. Shelly and Crawly were lucky that the gull couldn't fly well or high. That's all that saved them.'

'That and a brave fox and a mighty dog!' chirped Shelly.

The vet gave Mr Dog a final check-up too. 'I believe that this paw is healed,' she said. 'Are you going to keep him?'

'You know I take in a lot of strays. I look after them for as long as they need me.' Minnah smiled. 'Something tells me that no one gets to keep this dog!'

Mr Dog held up his healed paw to Minnah, and she took it for a gentle handshake. She had been a lovely pet human, but he knew she understood: he was a hound who could never be happy in one place. Not when there was such a big world to explore, and other animals who might need his help.

I suppose I'm a little bit wild at heart myself, thought Mr Dog.

The vet stayed to help the wildlife response team carefully catch the injured herring gull and her chick. Mr Dog watched to be sure they were both all right, and then, quietly, slipped away.

He roamed the streets of the city, back sticking to the shadows, sniffing about for Ferdy's trail. *It's a good job foxes have such a strong scent,* he thought.

But soon he realised where the smell-trail was leading him – straight back to Ryan's new neighbourhood!

Oh, no, thought Mr Dog. *Surely Ferdy can't be going back to Ryan after what happened last night?*

Mr Dog waited in the square park, out of sight in some bushes, keeping an eye on Ryan's house. The building was quiet and empty.

Hours passed and night fell. Then Ryan's van drove up and parked outside. Ryan got out and went through his red front door.

'Oh, no!' Mr Dog whimpered. 'What if Ryan has taken Ferdy far away again?'

He started forward from the bushes, ready to give

the van a good sniffing. Yes . . . sure enough, he *could* smell Ferdy! The smell was getting stronger . . .

'Hello, Mr Dog!' Ferdy poked his head out from underneath the van. 'Fancy seeing you here!'

Mr Dog gave a big doggy grin of relief. 'Hello to you too,' he said. 'But I did not fancy seeing you here.'

'Sorry to surprise you,' said Ferdy with a grin. 'I was hiding behind a tree and saw you sneaking over, so I came to meet you!'

'You really shouldn't stay this close to Ryan, you know. That part of your life has ended.'

'I know it has,' said Ferdy brightly. 'I came here to start *another* life . . .'

x

113

'With ME!' The next moment, Vix pushed

her head out from under the van beside him,

her single fang gleaming in the moonlight. 'I've

wanted a mate to hang around with for ages.

I reckon Ferdy and I will get along pretty well!'

'I think so too!' Ferdy nipped her playfully on the nose. 'We're going to leave this part of town and find a new place – just Vix and me.'

Vix nodded happily. 'We might even have cubs some day!'

'Well, I think a fresh start sounds like the perfect plan . . . For me too!' Mr Dog sat and held up a paw in farewell. 'I must find a new place, and new adventures. But one day I shall come back and see how you're getting on. Yes, I shall.' As he padded away, he looked back and gave his biggest doggy grin. 'You're not a faraway fox any more, Ferdy. From now on,

you're a *close-together* fox – and you'll stay that

way for always!'

Notes from the Author

A few years ago I found a tortoise in my back garden. I had no idea how it could have got there. The garden walls were too high for it to climb over them and it certainly couldn't have burrowed underneath. It was a mystery until I suddenly realised it must have been carried in by a fox.

Foxes are always on the look out for a tasty snack and will eat almost anything (even if a tortoise is just a bit too crunchy!). Having rescued the poor tortoise, I decided I should do my best to help so I put up a 'Lost Tortoise' notice and, luckily, found the owner. He lived miles away, and it turned out the tortoise had been missing for years. He was thrilled but very surprised to see it again! I hoped the poor tortoise hadn't been carried around by the fox for all that time.

Foxes are amazing animals (the grey fox in North

America can even climb trees). You can find them all over the world and they live not just in the countryside but also in towns and cities where they bring the wildness of nature right into the heart of our urban streets. I can spend hours watching them. For example, just take a look at their tails (known as brushes) – not only do they use them for balance (jumping over garden walls) but they will also use them to keep warm when the weather turns cold and to signal to other foxes. If you are lucky you might sometimes see in a garden or park or by a railway line at night a family of fox cubs at play. They are beautiful to watch.

Even though you certainly have to be careful if you have guinea pigs, rabbits or chickens (or a tortoise) when there are foxes around I like to think we can all try to live together in peace. Just remember, never give them food and keep the lid tightly closed on your dustbin!

Have you read Mr Dog's
other adventures?

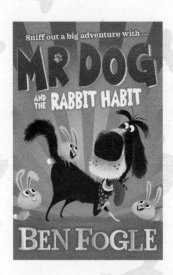

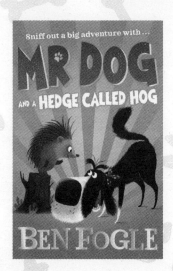